A SNOWLION'S LESSON
~A Tibetan Folk tale~

NORBU C. KHARITSANG

Paljor Publications

Many years ago there was a small, prosperous village at the foot of a beautiful snow mountain. Clear blue streams meandered through the village providing it with water for irrigation and for drinking. The times were good and everybody was rich and contended.

But there was one man named Tenzin in the village. He was a simple, poor man, and lived in a small thatched house at the far end of the village. He had a very rich friend named Tashi, who lived among the rich people of the village and owned many yaks, horses, and chickens. He was one of the richest men in the village. Instead of helping his poor friend, he always feared that his poor friend might one day become rich like himself.

Every day Tenzin would pack some food and go up the mountain to gather firewood, and sell them to the rich villagers to earn his living. No one knew how it came there, but there was a beautiful snowlion carved out of a rock in the mountain. Every day Tenzin would sit by the snowlion and eat his noon meal and talk to it. The food was neither good nor plenty but he would always put some in the snowlion's mouth and invite it to eat with him. This went on for many days.

One day as he put some food in the snowlion's mouth, it suddenly opened its mouth and said, "You are a kind-hearted man to share your food with me. I want to thank you and repay your kindness."

Tenzin was startled and a little frightened too.

"Do not be frightened, kind man. I only want to thank you and repay your kindness," said the snowlion.

Tenzin then gathered his courage and said, "Snowlion, you are a majestic animal but you are carved in stone and lonely. And I am poor and lonely too. It is pity that I cannot give you more food."

The snowlion said, "You are a kind man. You gave me what you could. Come here before sunrise tomorrow and bring a bag with you. I will give you something to take home."

Tenzin bade farewell to the snowlion and went home with a load of firewood. He did not tell anybody about his experience that day, not even to his rich friend. All night he wondered what the snowlion would give him to fill the bag.

Early next morning he went up the mountain with a small bag and some food. He also took his rope for firewood in case the snowlion did not give him anything.

As soon as Tenzin met the snowlion it greeted him, and said, "Do not waste time, kind man. You have a lot of work to do before the sun rises. Put your hand into my mouth. You will find gold in there. Fill your bag with my gold, but you must stop when the sun rises, otherwise I will shut my mouth tight and you will never be able to free yourself." Tenzin agreed to do as the snowlion said.

Tenzin put his hand into the snowlion's mouth and filled his small bag with gold. His bag was filled quickly. The snowlion told Tenzin that he could take some in his gown pouches too, but Tenzin was thankful for what he already got in his bag. Then the sun rose over the horizon and the snowlion closed its mouth.

Even with a bag full of gold, Tenzin still gathered some firewood and went home as usual. He counted and recounted the gold that night. When it was dawn, he hid the gold inside the hearth and covered them with ash and fire-wood.

Tenzin thought of all the things that he will do with the gold. He wanted to build a nice big house and marry a beautiful wife and have many children. Meanwhile, he went on gathering firewood, but now he did not gather so much firewood as before. The villagers wondered why the loads of firewood that he sold were smaller than before.

"Well, I am getting old and cannot carry as much as I used to," he told them.

One day he knocked down his small thatched house and built himself a nice big house. He filled it with many good things and bought many yaks, horses and chicken. He also married a beautiful wife. He was richer and happier than all the other people in the village. But he still lived at the far end of the village.

Soon everyone in the village was talking about Tenzin's sudden prosperity. His rich friend, Tashi, was jealous and curious too. So one day Tashi went to visit Tenzin.

"Friend, I am very happy that you are rich now. How did you get all the wealth?" Tashi asked.

"The snowlion carved in the rock in the mountain gave me a bag of gold," replied Tenzin honestly.

Tashi did not believe Tenzin. Nevertheless, he asked Tenzin to show him the way to the stone snowlion. When Tenzin showed him the way up to the mountain and to the stone snowlion, Tashi dressed himself as a poor man and went up the mountain to gather firewood.

Every day Tashi sat by the stone snowlion to eat his noon meal and gave it delicious foods. He thought if the snowlion gave so much gold in return for his poor friend's

meager food, the snowlion would definitely give him a lot more gold if he gave it plenty of good food. So each day he brought different delicious foods and fed the snowlion.

Even after feeding it for many days, the snowlion did not speak to him. He thought his friend had lied to him. Yet, he did not give up, and went up the mountain for many more days.

Then one day, the snowlion suddenly opened its mouth and thanked Tashi for his kindness and promised to repay him. Just as it had told Tenzin, the snowlion told him to come early in the morning with a bag.

He did not gather any firewood, and went home very excited. He could not wait for the day to be over. All night long he kept thinking about all the gold he would have.

Well before sunrise the next day, Tashi took a big bag and went up the mountain. As usual, he greeted the stone snowlion and put his big bag in front of the snowlion.

"Welcome," said the snowlion. "I want to repay your kindness with gold but you must hurry up, and don't be too greedy. You must do as I tell you."

"I will not be greedy and will do exactly as you tell me," said Tashi.

"There is gold in my mouth," said the snowlion. "Fill

your bag with my gold but you must stop before the sun rises; otherwise I will shut my mouth tight and you will never be able to free yourself."

When the snowlion opened its mouth, Tashi put his hand into its mouth and greedily scooped out gold as fast as he could. He went on filling his big bag. When the sun was almost over the horizon, his bag was only half filled.

The snowlion warned Tashi to stop, but he went on scooping out more gold. As the sun rose over the horizon, the snowlion closed its mouth. No matter how much he struggled, Tashi could not free his hand. He begged the stone snowlion to open its mouth once more, but it would not open its mouth at all.

Tashi pleaded for a long time, "Please release my hand, I want no more gold". All of sudden the snowlion released Tashi's hand, and all the gold he had gathered in his big bag also vanished.

Tenzin lived happily ever after, but his rich friend spent the rest of his life lamenting his greed.

The End

རྡོའི་སེང་གེས་ཁ་གདངས་པ།

༄༅། །སྟོན་མ་བཀྲིས་ཉེར་བའི་མི་ཕྱུག་པོ་ཞིག་དང་། བསྐུན་འཛིན་ཉེར་བའི་མི་སྐྱོ་པོ་ཞིག་ཡོད་པ་ རེད། བསྐུན་འཛིན་གྱི་ཉིན་ལྟར་ལྟ་རེ་དང་ཚལ་པ་ལྟོ་ཁད་གང་རེ་འཁྱུར་ནས་ཤིང་གཅོད་པར་རིའི་སྣང་ ལ་འགྲོ་གི་ཡོད་པ་རེད། རེ་དེའི་སྣང་ལ་རྡོའི་སེང་གེ་གཅིག་མ་གཏོགས་གཞན་སུ་ཡང་མེད་པ་རེད། ཉིན་ ལྟར་བསྐུན་འཛིན་གྱིས་གུང་ཚིགས་སྐབས་སྐུན་མཆེད་སེང་གེ་ལགས་ཞལ་ལག་ཏོག་ཚམ་མཆོད་དང་། ཞེས་ལབ་ཀྱི་ཡོད་པ་རེད། ཟླ་བ་ནས་ཟླ་བ། ལོ་ནས་ལོ་བར་བསྐུན་འཛིན་གྱིས་རྡོའི་སེང་གེ་དེ་ལ་ཞལ་ ལག་སྤྲད་པ་རེད།

ཉིན་གཅིག་བསྐུན་འཛིན་གུང་ཚིགས་སྐབས་སྐུན་མཆེད་སེང་གེ་ལགས་ཞལ་ལག་ཏོག་ཚམ་མཆོད་ དང་། ཞེས་ལབ་པ་དང་སྐྱོ་ཕྱུར་དུ་རྡོའི་སེང་གེ་དེས་ཁ་གདངས་ནས་ཕྱགས་རྗེ་ཆེ་སྤྱུན་མཆེད་སྐུན་འཛིན་ ཁྱེད་རང་མི་ཞི་དགས་སེམས་བཟང་པོ་ཞིག་འདུག ཁྱེད་རང་ལ་ལྟོ་ཚུང་ཅུང་ལམ་མེད་ཀྱང་ང་ལ་ བགོ་བཤའ་ཆག་ཁག་ཁག་བྱེད་ཀྱི་འདུག ང་ངས་ཁྱེད་ལ་གང་འདུ་བྱས་ནས་རྗེན་ལན་འཇལ་དགོས་ སམ། ཞེས་ལབ་མ་ཐག་བསྐུན་འཛིན་དོན་འབྱོར་ནས་གང་བཤད་འདི་བཤད་མ་ཐྲེ་པར་ལུས།

དེ་ནས་སེང་གེས་ཡང་སྐྱར་བཤད་དོན། ཁྱེད་རང་མི་དང་པོ་ཞིག་སོང་ཚང་སང་ཉིན་ཉི་མ་མ་ ཤར་གོང་ཚོ་ཕྱད་གཅིག་འཁྱེར་ནས་འདིར་ཤོག ཕན་བྱོགས་ཤིག་བྱུས་ཚིག་ཅེས་ལབ་པ་རེད། སང་ ཉིན་ཞིགས་པ་བསྐུན་འཛིན་གྱིས་རྣམ་ཀུན་ལྟར་རེ་དེའི་སྣང་ལ་འཛོགས་ནས་སེང་གེའི་འཁྲིས་ལ་སྟེབས་ པ་དང་། སྐུན་མཆེད་བསྐུན་འཛིན་ཁྱེད་རང་སྟེབས་ཡོད་པས། ངའི་ཁའི་ནང་ལ་ལག་པ་རྒྱས་ན་ཁྱེད་ རང་ལ་གསེར་རག་གི་རེད། ཁྱེད་རང་གི་ལྟོ་ཕད་དང་ལག་ཚོད་གོང་སོང་ལེན་ན་འགྲིགས་ཀྱི་རེད། ཡིན་ ཡང་ཉི་མ་མ་ཤར་གོང་ལ་ལག་པ་ཁའི་ནང་ནས་བཏོན་ཚར་བ་བྱེད་དགོས་ཞེས་ལབ་པ་རེད།

བསྐུན་འཛིན་གྱི་ལག་པ་སེང་གེའི་ཁའི་ནང་ལ་བཅུག་ནས་རང་གི་ལྟོ་ཕད་གང་ཚམ་གསེར་སྣངས་ པ་རེད། སྟོས་ཕད་ཅུང་ཅུང་དེ་མགྲོགས་པོ་ཁེས་ཚང་། ཨ་ཁ་ཁྱེད་རང་གི་ལྟོ་ཕད་ཆེ་རྩམ་ཞིག་ཁྱེར་

ཡོད་ཚོགས་ཀ། ཞེས་སེང་གེས་ལབ་པ་རེད། འདིས་དའི་མི་ཚོའི་རིང་འདང་གི་རེད། ཚེས་ལབ་ཚས་སེང་གེར་ཕྱགས་རྗེ་ཆེ་ཞུས་ནས་ཕྱིར་ལོག

གསེར་དེས་སྟོ་གོས་བཟང་དུ་ཕྱིན་པ་དང་། བསྟན་འཛིན་གྱིས་མནའ་མ་ཞིག་བསུས། ཁང་པ་ཡང་ཡག་པོ་ཞིག་རྒྱབ་པ་རེད། ཁོའི་གྲོགས་པོ་བཀྲིས་ཀྱི་སེམས་ལ་བསྟན་འཛིན་མགྱོགས་པོ་དེ་འདི་ཕྱུག་པོ་ག་འདྲ་བྱས་ནས་ཆགས་པ་ཡིན་ནམ་བསམ་ནས་སྐད་ཆ་དྲིས་དུས། བསྟན་འཛིན་གྱིས་རྗེའི་སེང་གེའི་ལོ་རྒྱུས་ཆ་ཚང་བཤད་པ་རེད། སད་ཞོགས་དེར་བཀྲིས་ཀྱིས་གོས་སྟི་པོ་ཞིག་གྱོན། སྐྲ་རེ་དང་ཙམ་པ་ཏོག་ཙམ་འཁུར་ནས་རི་དེའི་སྐེད་ལ་འཛེགས་པ་རེད། གུང་ཚིགས་ཀྱི་དུས་སུ་ཁོས་རྗེའི་སེང་གེ་དེའི་འཁྲིས་ལ་ཕྱིན་ནས་སྐུན་མཆེད་སེང་གེ་ལགས་ཞལ་ལག་ཏོག་ཙམ་བཞེས་དང་ཞེས་བསྟན་འཛིན་གྱིས་བྱས་པ་ནང་བཞིན་ལབ་པ་རེད།

ཉིན་གཅིག་སེང་གེས་ཁ་གྲགས་ཏེ་བསྟན་འཛིན་ལ་ལབ་པ་བཞིན་བགྱིས་ལ་བཀད་པས། བགྱིས་དགའ་ཐག་ཆོད་ནས་སང་ཞིག་སྟོ་ཕད་ཆེན་པོ་ཞིག་ཁྱེར་ནས་རྗེའི་སེང་གེ་ཡོད་ས་དེར་སྤེབས་དུས། ཁོའི་ནང་ལ་ལག་པ་རྒྱས་ནས་འདོད་རྔམ་ཆེན་པོས་གསེར་སྐང་པོ་ཡིན་པ་རེད། ཉི་མ་ཧར་གྲབས་ཡོད་པ་མ་ཤེས་པར། རྗེའི་སེང་གེ་ཁ་བཙུམ། བགྱིས་ཀྱི་ལག་པ་སེང་གེའི་ཁ་ནང་དུ་ཕོར་ཏེ་འཐེན་མ་ཐུབ། ཨ་ཙི་སེང་གེ་སྐུ་མཁྱེན། ཁ་གདོངས་རོགས་གནང་། ངས་གསེར་ཚང་མ་ཕྱིར་སྤྲོག་ཕྱེད་ཀྱི་ཡིན་ཞེས་ལབ་པ་དང་། ལས་སང་གསེར་རྣམ་ཡལ། བགྱིས་ཀྱི་ལག་པ་ཡང་སྦྱོད་པ་རེད།།

(བོད་གཞུང་ཤེས་རིག་པ་ཡུལ་བྱེས་པའི་བཙུན་དེབ་ ༡༩༨༡ འདོན་ཐེངས་ཨང་གྲངས་ ༣ ནས།)